Love You
Head to Toe

To Nori and Yeti

Love You
Head to Toe

—

Written and illustrated by **Ashley Barron**

Owlkids Books

Baby, you're a **sea star**,

Basking in the sun.

Wake up and stretch from head to toe.

Your day has just begun.

Baby, you're just like a kitten,

Reaching up so high,

Batting flutter-flits and whirlygigs.

Catch that butterfly!

You're just like a **duckling**,

Riding on my back.

Splishing and splashing around the pool,

Quack, quack, quack, quack, quack!

Baby, you're a **bear cub**,

Toddling on two feet.

Tip and tumble, down you fall,

In one big bear hug heap.

You're my little **hedgehog** baby,

When I wipe your bum.

Curled up in a hedgehog ball,

Until the cleanup's done.

You're my little penguin,

In the wintry weather.

Zipped and buttoned, bundled up,

Cozy and warm together.

Baby, you're just like a **chipmunk**,

When it's time for lunch.

Filling chubby chipmunk cheeks,

Messy as you munch.

Baby, you're just like a **joey**.
From mommy's pouch you peek,
Watching people passing by,
As we journey down the street.

You're just like a **turtle**, baby,

Scooting on all fours.

Dashing over sandy dunes,

To play along the shore.

You're my cheeky **monkey**.

Oo-oo-oo. Ee-ee.

Tiny fingers hold on tight.

One bar, two bar, three.

You're my sleepy **hippo**.

In the afternoon,

Your great big hippo yawn,

Tells me it's naptime soon.

Baby, you're just like a **froggy**,

Jumping on the spot.

Outstretched fingers, springy toes,

Giggling as you hop.

You're my little **otter** baby,

Bathing in the tub.

Holding treasures on your tummy,

As we rub-a-dub-dub.

You're my **snuggle bug** baby,

Such a joy to get to know,

From chipmunk cheeks to froggy feet,

I love you head to toe.

Owlkids Books acknowledges the financial support of the Canada Council for the Arts, the Ontario Arts Council, the Government of Canada through the Canada Book Fund (CBF) and the Government of Ontario through the Ontario Media Development Corporation's Book Initiative for our publishing activities.

Published in Canada by
Owlkids Books Inc.
1 Eglinton Avenue East
Toronto, ON M4P 3A1

Published in the United States by
Owlkids Books Inc.
1700 Fourth Street
Berkeley, CA 94710

Library of Congress Control Number: 2018944997

Library and Archives Canada Cataloguing in Publication

Barron, Ashley, author, illustrator
    Love you head to toe / written and illustrated by Ashley Barron.

ISBN 978-1-77147-304-0 (hardcover)
    I. Title.

PS8603.A7698L68 2019   jC811'.6   C2018-903192-1

Edited by: Debbie Rogosin
Designed by: Alisa Baldwin

The artwork in this book was created in paper collage, with some digital enhancements.

Manufactured in Shanghai, China, in September 2018, by C&C Joint Printing Co.
Job #HS4241

A   B   C   D   E   F

  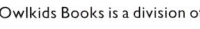 

Publisher of Chirp, Chickadee and OWL | Owlkids Books is a division of   Bayard CANADA
www.owlkidsbooks.com